Angela Dey

This book is dedicated to my mom, who has always encouraged my writing and saved every story I've ever written, even as a young child. And to my husband, who supports all (ok, most) of my crazy ideas. And thanks to his overflowing sock drawers, which prompted this story. This book wouldn't exist without either of you.

www.mascotbooks.com

Trixie Bixby and Her 66 Pairs of Socks

For more information, please contact:
Mascot Books
620 Herndon Parkway, Suite 320
Herndon, VA 20170
info@mascotbooks.com

Library of Congress Control Number: 2021917005

CPSIA Code: PRT1021A
ISBN-13: 978-1-63755-074-8

Printed in the United States

Trixie Bixby
and Her **66** Pairs of
SOCKS

Angela Delf
Illustrated by Chiara Civati

Trixie Bixby was a girl who had **66** pairs of socks.
With socks everywhere,
they were quite a disaster—she had a lot!

There were socks in her dresser, socks in her closet, and socks under her bed.
Trixie had socks that were **yellow**, socks that were **purple**, and socks that were **green** and **red**.

She had socks with polka dots, socks with stripes, and socks with kangaroos.

With so many options to pick from each day, it was a struggle for Trixie to choose!

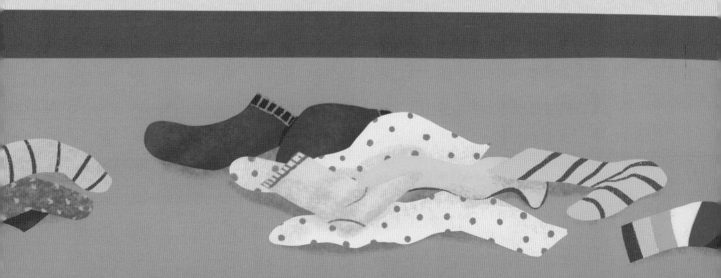

Her mom thought Trixie had too many socks,

but Trixie didn't think that was true.

Trixie liked knowing she had socks in **9** different

shades of her favorite color, **blue** .

Trixie loved her socks and didn't want to part

with any of her **66** pairs.

How could she choose between those

with the rainbows or those with the

brown teddy bears?

One day at school, Trixie noticed a girl, a new friend,
without any socks at all on her feet.
The girl said she didn't have any socks and looked
embarrassed as her face turned red as a beet.

Trixie wanted to help. After all, with so many socks,
she knew she had a few to share!
After school that day, Trixie went home and sorted her socks,
all the pairs that were there.

Trixie pulled out the fuzzy socks, the socks with the shapes, and the extra pair that were green. She could part with the pair that had pictures of cones of ice cream.

Trixie put the socks for her friend in a bag and packaged it up with a bow.

All in all, Trixie shared **14** pairs of socks with her new friend—enough for **2** weeks in a row!

Trixie liked the warm feeling she felt when she shared.
She counted the socks that were left,
and she still had **52** pairs!

Trixie decided to give more socks away to those who needed them more.

Her mom started to notice the bags of socks that were lining up by the door.

When Trixie's mom asked her about the bags,
she shrugged and said she was able to share.
After all, Trixie still had so many socks,
she still had plenty to spare.

Trixie noticed that getting dressed each morning was going much faster.
This was because her sock drawer was no longer such a disaster!

While sharing her extra socks,

Trixie helped herself feel good too.

Now, she has just the right number of socks . . .

and her favorites are still the ones that are **blue**.

THE
END

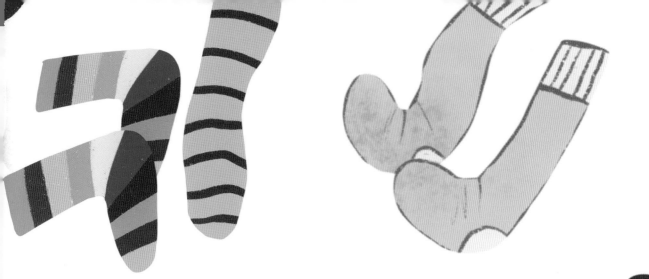

About the Author

Angela lives in Wisconsin with her husband and three children. After more than a decade in the financial services industry, she decided to stay at home with her children. As she was constantly looking for ways to declutter, organize, and simplify her life at home, this book was born. In addition to writing, she enjoys reading, running, coaching soccer, volunteering at her children's school, and traveling. An avid supporter of her library and sharing things she no longer needs, she enjoys stocking her little free library, painting and hiding inspirational rocks for people to find (#ricelakerocks), and donating to others.